The Travels of J. B. Rabbit

Written and Illustrated by
Doris Susan Smith

Publishers · GROSSET & DUNLAP · New York

Library of Congress Catalog Number: 82-80876. ISBN: 0-448-16585-6

Printed in Belgium by Offset Printing Van den Bossche. Published simultaneously in Canada.

Dear J.B.,

Now that you have settled down in your new burrow, what would you say to a few days at the seashore with a comfortable bed, good food, and fantastic fishing?

The wind is light, the weather fair, and it's the beginning of the lobster season. Don't waste a minute! Come right away, and telephone your arrival time from the station before you leave.

Cheers!

As ever,
Your Cousin Waldo

P.S. There is a good night train!

Jeremy B. Rabbit had never been to the seashore and felt that he needed a vacation. Off he scampered to the tool burrow, and after much rummaging around, he found his fishing rod neatly packed away in a corner.

Out came the traveling bag from under his bed, and in went his bathrobe, bedroom slippers, toothbrush and toothpaste, whisker cream, and his favorite bedtime books. All this was carefully stowed away with his alarm clock and the sailor blouse Waldo had sent him for Christmas.

In the kitchen he prepared and packed a delicious picnic with a thermos of hot carrot soup.

Jeremy then tidied up his burrow, closed the shutters, and carefully locked the door.

It was a hot walk to the station. Luckily, Mole was resting in the shade at his favorite spot under the signpost, and Jeremy gave him his keys as he always did before going away on a trip.

"Afternoon Mole. Here are my keys," said Jeremy. "I am off to see my Cousin Waldo who lives by the sea."

Being a mole of few words, Mole nodded and smiled goodbye.

Jeremy arrived at the station long before the train was due. He had plenty of time to purchase his ticket and buy a bag of his favorite fudge, as well as a magazine with lots of pictures.

The waiting room was almost empty as he sat down on a bench to read. But Jeremy was so excited that he could hardly sit still, and he soon put aside his magazine and even forgot to taste the fudge.

The train finally puffed into the station only five minutes behind schedule. Jeremy found a window seat opposite a small guinea pig and his mother, and settled himself down comfortably with a sigh of relief. The engine whistled twice, the conductor raised his hand, and off they went.

Through the window, Jeremy could see the woods and fields slide by as they huffed and clattered across the countryside.

"I am going to Grandmother's," piped a squeaky voice. "Where are you going Mr. Rabbit?"

Jeremy realized that the little guinea pig was speaking to him. "I am going to the seashore to visit my Cousin Waldo," he replied.

"Oh!" said the small guinea pig, and he added, "Are you hungry? I am."

Jeremy admitted that he was, and Mrs. Guinea Pig smiled. Soon both picnic baskets were unpacked, and a delightful picnic supper was underway.

Later when it was dark and the supper things had been packed away, Jeremy sat back in his seat and closed his eyes contentedly. Soon he was dreaming of sparkling waves and glistening dolphins.

Early next morning, Jeremy woke up just as the train jolted to a stop. There was Waldo on the platform, and Jeremy had just enough time to grab his things and jump out before the engine's whistle blew and the train started off again.

"Glad to see you, Old Salt. Didn't come a minute too soon. Throw your gear onto the back seat of old Betsy and climb in," said Waldo in his gruff and gravelly voice.

Waldo turned the crank, and Betsy coughed and wheezed a few times before sputtering to life.

"Glad to have you aboard!" shouted Waldo as he took the wheel. "How about a spot of breakfast down by the harbor before going to the house?"

Out beyond the busy harbor lay the shimmering sea. There was so much to look at that Jeremy didn't know where to start. The sea breeze was salty and fresh with the promise of all sorts of exciting things to do out on the water.

Breakfast was delicious. Jeremy could hardly believe that it wasn't all a dream and that soon he would wake up back in his burrow!

Overhead the gulls wheeled and glided on the breeze uttering little piercing cries.

"If you've finished eating," said Waldo, "we'll be on our way."

"There she is!" called out Waldo, as they came to a turn in the road. Overlooking the sea was a little house of wood and glass perched on the rocky shore.

Waldo showed Jeremy his room, which had a berth for a bed—just like on a ship. There was no porthole, however, but a large window instead, opening onto the sea.

Down below was a small dock and there, gently tugging at the ropes, was a splendid fishing boat.

"That's the **Swordfish**," said Waldo proudly. "Let's take her out for a spin."

Jeremy soon found his sea legs and began to enjoy himself. After a while the little boat turned and chugged back close to the shore. Waldo dropped anchor and said, "What would you say to a bit of scuba diving?"

He then proceeded to change himself into the strangest creature Jeremy had ever seen.

After this extraordinary experience, Jeremy went diving every morning with Waldo. One day, however, the sky was overcast and the sea gray and choppy.

"Let's go to the beach," suggested Waldo, "and dig for clams."
On another day, Waldo and Jeremy found mussels and
shrimp. And one day, Jeremy found his first starfish.

One night Waldo cooked a seafood dinner, and Jeremy had his best meal ever! He had never tasted such delicious food—and to think it all came from the sea.

Waldo told tall tales of the fish he had caught, and after dinner, he showed Jeremy a ship in a bottle. But in spite of Waldo's explanations, Jeremy couldn't understand how such a big ship came to be in such a small bottle!

"Tomorrow we will go out to raise the lobster pots and do some fishing now that you've got your sea legs" announced Waldo.

GO UP IN A BALLOON

As they set off next morning, an airplane trailing a banner flew by.

"Go up in a balloon," muttered Waldo. "Sounds interesting."

SWORDFISH

At the lobster grounds, Waldo lifted the pots and threw the lobsters to Jeremy. Jeremy quickly popped them into the baskets before they could nip him.

Suddenly it became very windy and the waves began to get choppy. Then it started to pour.

"We'd better get home fast," shouted Waldo.

GO UP IN A BALLOON

SWORDFISH

Just when the sea was at its roughest, the **Swordfish's**
engine failed. Poor Jeremy huddled in the deckhouse, wet and
cold and frightened.

All at once, he pointed across the waves. "Dolphins!" he
cried.

"You're right, Old Salt," said Waldo, "Dolphins love the
rough weather. Say," he added, "if we could get a line to them
they might tow us home."

"I'll hold the boat steady," bellowed Waldo above the roar of the wind, and you get a line out."

"What do you mean? What's a line? How…"

"Stop asking questions," roared Waldo. "Pick up that rope, go to the stern, and throw it out. And get a move on. The dolphins won't wait forever."

Clutching the rope in soaking paws and lurching all over the place as the boat pitched and tossed, Jeremy made for the stern and hurled out the rope. It landed in the sea, yards from the nearest dolphin.

"No good! Try again," shouted Waldo.

This time the dolphin leaped in the air and caught the rope in his strong jaws.

Help! We're going backwards," shrieked Jeremy.

"Idiot! Give him time. He knows what he's doing," Waldo grumbled. His patience with Jeremy was running out.

Slowly the dolphin swam through the waves, heading away from the stern towards the bow. The **Swordfish** rolled dangerously.

"He'll never do it," wailed Jeremy.

Suddenly the little ship jerked forward.

"I knew he could do it!" Waldo shouted, and slowly they headed for home.

Waldo was rather sorry he had gotten so angry. He smiled. "Well done, J.B.," he said. "I'm sure glad you can throw straight."

As they tied up at the jetty, the sun came out and the wind died down. Jeremy was so grateful to the dolphin for saving his life that he leaned over and kissed him. Waldo grabbed hold of Jeremy's slicker.

"Don't fall overboard now," he said.

Back home, Jeremy rubbed himself dry. "That was a real adventure," Jeremy said cheerfully. "I'm glad I've been out in a storm **once**."

But Waldo was already thinking about the next day. "Tomorrow," he said, "we'll go up in a balloon!"

The weather the next day was perfect for ballooning. Waldo bought their tickets at the entrance to the balloon grounds. Then Jeremy and Waldo chose a red and pink balloon. They stepped into the basket and soon were up in the air.

Jeremy loved it. "Oh, look!" he called. "There's a pig down there waving to us."

Waldo decided not to look down.

"I can see the train I came in," Jeremy called out. "And the harbor, and the lighthouse, and look—there's your house."

"I can see the sea," said Waldo wistfully. "I think we'll go fishing tomorrow...."

Dear Cousin Waldo,

   I'm not very good at writing thank-you letters,
so this will have to be short.
   I had a wonderful vacation, and I'm glad you
invited me. I loved the fishing, and the scuba
diving, and that exciting storm. I really wasn't
frightened. And the balloon trip was the greatest
thing that's ever happened to me.
   Remember the sailor blouse you gave me for
Christmas? I wear it all the time to remind me of
the best holiday I ever had in my whole life.

                    Your grateful cousin,
                    J.B.

P.S.   Give my love to the dolphin.

P.P.S. When are you coming here for a taste of
        country life?